DREAMWORKS

the BAD
GUYS

A VERY BAD HOLIDAY

DreamWorks

the BAD GUYS

A VERY BAD HOLIDAY

By Kate Howard

Scholastic Inc.

DreamWorks The Bad Guys: A Very Bad Holiday © 2023 DreamWorks Animation LLC. All Rights Reserved.

ISBN 978-1-339-02379-3

10 9 8 7 6 5 4 3 2 1   23 24 25 26 27

Printed in the U.S.A.   40

First printing 2023

Book design by Ashley Vargas

'Twas the day before Christmas,
   Before the Bad Guys turned good,
When all through the city,
   They cased each and every neighborhood.

Did that rhyme? Is "twas" even a word?
Look, here's the thing: Our story is set when the
Bad Guys were still bad.
Okay?
And at the best time of year, when all the good heists
can be had . . .

CHAPTER ONE

The city was bursting with Christmas spirit. Festive garlands hung merrily from all the buildings, and cheerful green wreaths dotted the space between each sturdy lamppost that lined the downtown streets. Hot, hazy sun shone down on the holiday decorations, baking the greenery until the air was rich with the scent of pine. It reeked of Christmas—in the best possible way.

People were smiling, and the air was filled with good cheer. The holidays made *everyone* happy.

But there was no one more excited about the scents and sights of the holiday season than the notorious Bad Guys. Because Christmas was the time of year when they had executed some of their very best heists of all time.

For many, Christmas is known as a time of giving. For the Bad Guys, it's the best possible time for them to *take*.

"Alright, guys," Wolf howled joyfully from the driver's seat of their snazzy getaway car. He glanced into the passenger and back seats, flashing a toothy smile at the pals riding in the car with him: Snake, Piranha, Webs, and Shark. The five of them were known far and wide as the Bad Guys, and this bunch loved nothing more than to live up to that name. Wolf adjusted his paws on the wheel and whipped the car around a corner. "What's tomorrow?"

Wolf's pals all shouted, "The Bad Guys Holiday Heist-tacular!"

"And what does that mean?" Wolf asked them with a killer grin. He swerved to avoid some of the people who were lining up along the edge of the street for the holiday parade. The crowds stuffed into town added some extra excitement to that day's drive.

✦ Possible Names for the Bad Guys' ✦
Ultimate Holiday Heist

Wreck the Halls

Jingle Bell Bank Heist

Makin' It Rein(deer)

Mistletoe Mayhem

Rockin' around the Banking Tree

Rudolph and the Red-Nosed Robbers

Twelve Days of Heists

I'm Dreaming of a Gold Kwanzaa

Holly Jolly Hanukkah Heist

Santa Claus Is Comin' to Get Your Stuff

Silent Night Sneak Attack

How the Bad Guys Stole Christmas

Feliz Navidad, Fools!

Chrome for the Holidays

Frosty the No-Man

Let It Snow . . . Cash, Cash, Cash

Winter Wonder-Where-It-Went?

Bad Guys Holiday Heist-tacular ★

The team's tech-wizard tarantula, Webs, glanced out at the crowds of unsuspecting ordinary people and began to explain the plan. "While all these normies stay home with their loved ones or whatever—"

Piranha cut her off to excitedly blurt out, "This place turns into a ghost town!" He wriggled with excitement. "No guards. No fuzz."

Shark giggled and said, "No late shift employees peeping for burglars." Rubbing his fins together, he cheered, "The city's our heisting stage!"

Snake hissed, "And we're gonna clean it out." He looked out of the car window at all the smiling fools. Fools who had no idea that, once again, the Bad Guys had a whole lot of surprises in store for their precious city on Christmas morning.

Wolf chuckled to himself. "It's a Bad Guys tradition," he mused. Gripping the steering wheel, he wiggled his bushy eyebrows and said, "And so is spending the day *before* coming up with a list of everything we're going to steal on Christmas morning."

Piranha's eyes went wide as their car swerved past a row of shops. "Ooh!" he said, bouncing up and down in the back seat. "I wanna hit that place with all the stinky cheese." He snickered and said, "No reason! I don't even *like* it." The other guys glanced over, giving him suspicious looks. His pals were all pretty good at being able to tell when Piranha was telling a lie (in fact, thanks to his nervous farting, the gang could usually *smell* when he was telling a lie, too). Piranha blurted out, "Okay, I like it a *little!*"

Nodding, Wolf said, "Cheesy Dan's is on the list."

There weren't many places in the city that *weren't* on the hit list. While everyone else was tucked into their houses, celebrating Christmas morning together, the whole town would be theirs for the taking. Today was the perfect chance to scope out the options, and

List of Targets We're Going to Hit During the
BAD GUYS HOLIDAY HEIST-TACULAR

❄

Cheesy Dan's
Ruby's Diamond Dealers
Golden Goodies
Gettin' Wiggy With It (for Shark)
The City's Largest Jewelry Store
Kitchen Goodies & More
Eli's Electronics Emporium
Vases & Lampshades R Us
Fancy Art Museum
Police Station (nab Chief's microwave)
Cash, Cash, CASH at City Corporate Bank
Bonus: Steal a giant parade balloon? (Why not?)

tomorrow they would have all day to heist in peace.

Wolf steered the car carefully through more crowds of people who were waiting for the holiday parade to start. Little kids bounced eagerly in line for shaved ice treats, clusters of friends waved and shouted greetings to each other, and still others admired the holiday greenery and twinkle lights that made the whole city feel like a magical winter wonderland—even though the weather was typically sunny and warm.

Shark pointed as they zipped past another shop. "I could use some new wigs!"

Wolf swerved, expertly guiding the car through the jam-packed city. "Wig store," he said with a nod. "Got it!"

Suddenly, the crowds of people gathered on the sidewalks began to cheer wildly. Wolf glanced up, noticing that the huge Santa balloon was now soaring high in the sky several streets away, floating merrily along above all the people. Everyone's attention was drawn to the magnificent red-and-white balloon smiling down at them from the clear blue sky.

Wolf smirked as he noticed a man saluting the Santa balloon with actual *tears* in his eyes. Man, people were such *suckers* for that big guy in a red suit!

Out on a street corner, the chirpy news reporter, Tiffany Fluffit, was practically jumping up and down with excitement. "Tiffany Fluffit here!" she cried into her microphone as she smiled at the camera. "With the moment we've all been waiting for. Our beloved Big Nick has just made his first appearance! I think I speak for the entire city when I say . . ." She gazed lovingly up into the sky, grinning at the giant, air-filled Santa. "I love you, Big Nick!"

The Santa balloon sailed through the air, its handlers guiding it down the street toward City Corporate Bank. From the other direction, the Bad Guys were *also* heading toward the city center. Not to see the Big Nick balloon, like everyone else, but rather to scope out their favorite heist target.

"City. Corporate. Bank," Snake whispered, practically drooling as Wolf steered the car in the direction of their ultimate target. He slowed the car so the Bad Guys could all ogle their favorite building in the whole world. A guard—whose nametag read GARY—stood outside the main doors, carefully watching for trouble. He didn't notice the Bad Guys as they slowly cased the joint.

Wolf sighed happily. "That's what we've been waiting all year for," he said with a smile. "It's gonna be the cherry on top of our criminal sundae. Tomorrow morning, the bank—and everything else in this city—will be ours."

Snake lifted his tail to give his best bud a knowing fist-tail bump. The other Bad Guys whooped, sounding like a bunch of kids who were about to unwrap the greatest gift of all time.

Wolf revved the engine and shot forward. They'd seen enough for today. He felt ready for the next day's adventure. Now it was time to get home and rest up for the heist of the century first thing in the morning.

They were ready. Nothing could possibly go wrong.

CHAPTER TWO

It should have all been fine.

Good, even.

No biggie . . . really.

But unfortunately, someone spotted them. "It's the Bad Guys!" yelled a voice from the crowd. Other people noticed them and began to point and scream. Wolf knew it was time to hit it.

"Better get a move on it, Wolfie," Snake said.

As they zipped past the Santa that was being guided through the streets, Wolf accidentally swerved a little too close to the balloon.

Wolf could *totally* have avoided the problem . . . if only that one balloon handler hadn't decided to jump out of the way. But when that handler *did* jump out of the way, that's when one of the balloon ropes got tangled up in the Bad Guys' getaway car. As Wolf sped away from the scene, the *rest* of Santa's ropes got pulled out of the other balloon handlers' hands as well.

And *now* the giant Santa balloon was cruising down the street high above Wolf and his pals, attached to the bumper of the Bad Guys' getaway car. This was definitely *not* part of their plan.

"I think we just stole Santa?" Shark said.

"Niiiiice," Webs muttered.

"The Bad Guys are stealing Big Nick!" someone screamed. "Help! Somebody stop them!"

"That's not very good," Wolf said, looking up from the inside of the convertible, scoping out their new passenger high up in the sky. Stealing the Santa balloon had definitely not been on today's to-do list. And the big guy didn't look very jolly to be along for the ride.

"Uh . . . this isn't that famous balloon everybody is

freakishly emotionally attached to, is it?" Piranha asked, even though he kind of already knew the answer to his own question. This was *obviously* the same Santa balloon. It's not like there were a bunch of *other* giant Santa balloons floating around downtown on the day before Christmas.

"No," Snake said with a roll of his eyes. "This is a different giant Santa-shaped balloon."

Piranha sagged with relief.

Snake glared at him and said, "Of *course* it is!" He leaned out of the car's window to try to untangle the ropes stuck in their car bumper. But the ropes were really stuck.

Wolf slammed his foot on the gas, swerving wildly to try to shake the balloon loose. But nothing worked to set Santa free. Instead, Wolf's crazy driving just bopped the giant balloon around in the air, causing Santa to bounce to and fro between the city's tall buildings.

Parade-goers screamed as Wolf careened around the corner and sent Santa slamming into a giant building. Then another. And another. Santa slammed from side to side, then flew high up into the air—dragging the back of the Bad Guy mobile up into the air along with him. Seconds later, the car crashed back down, yanking Santa along with it. Big Nick slammed down on top of Wolf's car, smothering the Bad Guys under the giant balloon.

"I can't see!" Wolf yelped.

"Get it offa me!" Snake wailed.

"Ew," Shark whined. "I'm touching Santa's eyeball!"

"Who turned out the lights?" Webs yelped.

"Can we keep him?" Piranha begged.

Wolf shook off the balloon just enough that he could see the road ahead of him. He spotted a streetlight up ahead, and that's when he got an idea for how to fix their current problem. He slammed his foot down on the accelerator, bringing the car up to max speed. As they zipped past the traffic light, one of the balloon's ropes snagged the pole. Wolf nudged the gas a little more, and as they raced away, the Santa balloon was finally tugged loose.

"Ha!" Wolf whooped. "See ya, Santa!"

If they'd stuck around, they would have seen what happened next with their own eyes.

But in their rush to get away, the Bad Guys missed *all* the drama that came next.

The broken streetlight suddenly began to spark. Wires fizzled. And then, moments after the Bad Guys' car swerved and squealed away around the corner, the giant Santa balloon went up in flames.

CHAPTER THREE

"Christmas is canceled," Tiffany Fluffit wailed into her microphone. The cameraman sobbed quietly behind his camera. Nearby, children screamed and cried. Parents tried to comfort their kids, but everyone—adults *and* kids—was having a hard time getting the image of the burning Santa out of their minds. Especially since the burning balloon had been blown into the side of a building and got stuck there. Now the grisly face of a charred Santa was staring down at the city like a giant scary billboard.

"This is Tiffany Fluffit reporting live from the scene of the *worst* attack on this city since the introduction of electric scooters," Tiffany sobbed. She gathered herself together; this was a time to be professional, after all. "Our beloved Big Nick has been *destroyed* by the notoriously notorious Bad Guys. We're a city in mourning this morning."

The cameraman panned over the scene, getting raw, live footage of people's sadness.

"Why?!" someone sobbed.

"Why, indeed," Tiffany said into her microphone, dragging the camera's lens back her way. She shook her head miserably, frowned, then went on, "It's a senseless act of bah-humbuggery." She gestured to the side of the building, sighing as the camera captured footage of the city's useless attempt to wash the burned Santa off. "All attempts to wash the abomination off have only made it more terrifying, further lowering holiday spirits."

No matter how much water they sprayed at the side of the building, nothing worked. It seemed as if the building would forever be charred with the image of the horrifyingly melted Santa balloon.

"It's never felt less like Christmas in the city," Tiffany said sadly. She scanned the people surrounding her on the street, all of whom were going miserably about their usual business. She spotted Gary, the bank's guard, gazing up at the burned Santa wall. "Sir," the news reporter blurted out, shoving the microphone into his face. "Your reaction?"

Gary shook his head. "It's just not the holidays without Big Nick," he said gloomily. "He was like a father to me. Don't think I'll even celebrate tomorrow." Gary hung his head and shrugged. "Probably just go into work, guard the bank like any other day . . ." He choked back a sob and glanced up at the building. "I'll be extra attentive to my job guarding the bank, to distract myself from this monstrosity." He stared at the remnants of the burned balloon in horror. "Why can't I look away?"

Christmas just wouldn't be Christmas without Big Nick.

It was beginning to look like the Bad Guys Holiday Heist-tacular wasn't going to be so heist-tacular after all . . .

CHAPTER FOUR

"This can't be happening," Wolf wailed as he and his friends watched the evening news later that same day. They'd left the parade route thinking all was well. The Santa had been freed from the Bad Guys' car, people could move on with their holiday shopping and parade-watching, and Christmas could go forward as planned.

But then everything had gone wrong because of one annoying, broken streetlight! What were the odds that Big Nick would go up in flames?

The odds were *low*, those were the odds. But today, those odds seemed to be stacked against the Bad Guys.

"The whole point of Christmas morning is that no one is around to stop us from maximum heisting!" Piranha screamed as he glared at the TV.

Snake's head drooped. "But—but—we were going to rob the bank! And now we can't because of some dumb Santa?!"

"You take that back right now!" Webs snapped. "Santa is a criminal hero who deserves our respect, in balloon form or otherwise." Snake glared at her, so Webs explained, "He's broken into more homes than anyone, and he's *never* been caught!"

Snake rolled his eyes. That wasn't exactly on the same level as the stuff that they—the Bad Guys—had done during their illustrious criminal careers.

Piranha sobbed, then screamed, as he cycled through emotion after emotion. First he was angry, then he sunk into depression, and then he finally shouted out, "What's even the point of anything?" He flopped miserably onto the couch in their lair, then just as suddenly perked up. "Unless . . ." he glanced around at his buddies and said, "And hear me out on this: If we set our clocks back twenty-four hours and go to sleep right now, maybe when we wake up, none of this will have happened. Yeah?" He grinned desperately, showing his rows and rows of dagger-sharp teeth. "C'mon. Night, night." He closed his eyes and began to fake-snore softly.

Shark dropped his fins on his buddy's shoulders and told Piranha, "You're experiencing the five stages of heist-loss. Don't worry, we'll get through this together."

Piranha stared up at his pal, tears streaming down his face. "There's nothing to get through," he blubbered. "EVERYTHING IS FINE! I haven't been counting down the days since our last Holiday Heist-tacular. I'm not crying. *You're* crying!"

Wolf stepped in front of the two of them, hoping to stop Piranha's spiraling emotions from spinning even further out of control. "Look," he said calmly. "If destroying that Santa balloon was all it took to cancel

The Five Stages of Heist-Loss

Anger
Depression
Bargaining
Denial
~~Acceptance~~

NO! The Bad Guys NEVER
accept a heist-loss!

Christmas, then all we have to do is re-create it and—*boom!* Christmas is back!"

Webs whooped to get the gang's attention. Her *whoop* sounded like an air horn and it was a surprisingly loud sound coming from a tarantula. "That's the sound of all our problems being solved," she informed her crew with a cunning grin. "Because I've already made something better . . ."

CHAPTER FIVE

Along the river basin, Wolf, Snake, Shark, and Piranha stared at the giant, metal *thing* with their mouths hanging open. Wolf cocked his head, realizing immediately that the metal creation Webs had built was actually a large mechanical robot designed to look just like a muscle-bound Santa. *What* it was, was obvious. *Why* she'd built it was another matter.

"Roboclaus! Built this bad boy for our Christmas morning bank heist," Webs explained. "The security bars will be no match for this mechanical Santa's super strength. I was going to surprise you all tomorrow, but you can call me a genius *now*." Webs grinned at them, awaiting the team's praise.

"It is *surprising*, that's for sure," Wolf mused.

Webs nodded. "The normies will forget all about their precious Santa balloon once they lay their eyes on this beauty. It captures Santa's true nature." She cocked her head in the other direction, studying the surly and somewhat frightening-looking Santa. "None of that jolly business."

Webs typed a code on her computer, and moments later, Roboclaus raised his arm as if to wave. But instead of a jolly wave, flames shot out of his hand. With a shriek, Piranha jumped out of the way to avoid being cooked into a blackened filet.

"Hmm," Webs said thoughtfully. "Okay, that was supposed to make him dance, but it was still pretty awesome. The suit really should be operated by a driver." She nudged Wolf and added, "C'mon, Wolfie, try him on."

"Oh, that's—" Wolf began, backing away just a few tiptoed steps. He didn't really want to be the guy operating Webs's Santa mech. "I'm good. Thanks, though. And as great as . . . *this* is, the jolly component of Jolly Old Nick is probably why noncriminal folks like him."

Webs hopped up onto Roboclaus's shoulder and whispered into his ear, "Don't listen to him. You're perfect."

Wolf held up his paws, trying to think and see if he could come up with other ideas on the spot. Surely, this terrifying Roboclaus was not going to fill the hole left in peoples' hearts when they'd destroyed the real Santa balloon. "If we all work together," he said confidently, "I'm sure a bunch of criminal masterminds like us can make one silly Santa balloon."

How hard could it be to create a perfect replica of the jolly old Santa balloon?

The Bad Guys jumped right to work, gathering up as many materials as they could think of, hoping to build something that might trick the public into un-canceling Christmas. They sewed sheets together, painted the sheets red, and bustled to and fro, building the best homemade Santa they could.

"Even *I'm* a little offended by this," Snake said, when they'd finally finished, and everyone stepped back to admire their work.

Webs covered Roboclaus's eyes, hoping not to scare him with their awful creation.

Piranha announced, "His beard looks like a tentacle. I feel scandalized."

Wolf's face fell. This was obviously going to be harder than he'd originally thought.

But Bad Guys didn't give up. Ever. Even when a task seemed utterly impossible.

CHAPTER SIX

"Okay," Wolf said, clapping to get everyone's attention a bit later. He'd gathered the team at the heist board. It was brainstorming time. "We lost some time there, but we'll just have to figure out another way to cheer up the city in time to rob it on Christmas morning." He shrugged. "Which, sure, is in, like, twelve hours . . . so, lay it on me. What else says holiday spirit?"

"Stealing whatever we want because normally guards take the day off," Snake muttered. "But no, not this year. They'll be at work, ruining the only good thing about Christmas . . ."

"Only good thing? Are you kidding?" Shark gasped. "What about all the classic Christmas criminals?" He began testing out some of his favorite holiday disguises, knowing the team would be very impressed by all his options. "The Grinch?" he asked, sporting a puffy green wig.

Then he jammed a bowler hat on and said, "Hans Grouper?"

The gang didn't seem all that impressed. Shark knew it was time to debut his masterpiece. He tossed on a top hat and sideburns and blurted out, "And the OG of them all: Ebenezer Scrooge!"

The rest of the Bad Guys oohed and aahed. Piranha nodded. "That guy's a legend. He parties with ghosts and wears a dress to bed."

"And yet," Shark said, holding up a fin. "His story has never been properly told. So, I propose that we put on a show for the whole city, with me as Scrooge, and all the other characters, but without that needy, nefarious Tiny Tim tearing Scrooge down."

Wolf's eye twitched. He was trying really hard to

keep it together, but they were getting a little *too* off course here. "I would buy a ticket to that show," he told Shark, trying to keep his buddy happy. "*But* . . . we gotta stick to all the awful stuff people like—ahhh!" He cut off as he noticed the giant eyeball of the charred Santa balloon staring at them from just outside the window of their living room. It was as though the annoyingly jolly guy was watching them, *judging* them. Wolf quickly reached over and closed the shades.

"My favorite part of the holidays," Piranha mused, "Is getting a lump of coal. Really makes me feel like I'm making good choices."

The other Bad Guys nodded their heads in agreement. "The Naughty List is a badge of honor," Shark said in a hushed whisper.

"Maybe we can get everyone some coal?" Piranha suggested.

Wolf whooped. "Piranha, you're a genius."

"I am?" Piranha asked. He was confused. It was a good idea, but it wasn't exactly a *great* idea.

Wolf snapped and said, "*We're* going to play Santa!"

Snake eyed him suspiciously. "Let me get this straight. Are you suggesting we *give* instead of *take*?"

"Think of it this way," Wolf said. "We'll *steal* the gifts from the big department store and then *break into houses* to leave them!"

Snake narrowed his eyes. "That sounds a lot like Robin Hood, who is notoriously *good*."

"Ugh," Webs groaned. "That guy is the worst. He ruined tights for me."

Wolf shook his head. "We're only doing good for the greater *bad*. If folks have presents waiting for them, they'll stay home on Christmas morning . . . and our Holiday Heist-tacular can live again!"

Slowly, Snake began to nod his agreement. It made

Santa's Naughty List

Wolf: Ultimate Bad Guy . . . the man with the plan and all-out NAUGHTY
(in the very best way)

Shark: Master of Disguise

Tarantula (aka Webs): Tech-Spinning Wizard

Piranha: Loose cannon with a short fuse

Snake: Serpentine safe-cracking machine

sense, in a sort of crazy way. The *good* kind of crazy. The *Bad Guys'* kind of crazy. Brilliant.

Webs lifted one of her eight legs and said, "We also have to deal with this." She hopped onto the radio and turned it on. A blast of loud, angry heavy metal music blared out of the speakers. "After the balloon . . . uh, *incident*, the radio station stopped playing Christmas music and is instead broadcasting something called—"

Annoyed, Snake flicked the radio back off, dropping the room into silence. For a second, Webs didn't notice that the music was off, and so she continued to yell, "—'DOOM TUNES' instead." She cleared her throat and lowered her voice to a normal level once again. "This music isn't helping with holiday spirit. If someone could get into the recording studio to help, I could hack the station's antenna and stream my sweet Santa mix."

Wolf turned back to the heist board. He was in full-on planning mode now. He began to sketch out the plan—they had the start of something good. "Alright, guys," he said with a devious smirk. "Let's go do some *good*, so we can be *bad*."

CHAPTER SEVEN

That night, the Bad Guys put their *new* plan into motion. Wolf checked the master plan one last time with the gang, to make sure everyone knew their part. The ultimate goal, he reminded the crew, was to bring holiday spirit back to the city—so that *they* could bring on some holiday *heisting*!

He explained each piece of the plan. "First, Piranha will help Webs get to the antenna so she can hack it." Up on the rooftop of the radio station, Webs and Piranha got ready to set the first pieces into place.

"Then," Wolf continued, "Shark will infiltrate the radio station and distract the DJ so she doesn't notice Webs is taking over the feed with holiday music." Inside the station, Shark was wearing a top hat, ready for his task.

But the best gig of all was saved for Snake and Wolf. They were dressed in Santa hats, so they could get right into character. "Finally," Wolf finished up, "Snake and I will steal gifts from the department store to then break in and leave at unsuspecting houses."

Once everyone was in position, Wolf signaled for them to go.

At the entrance to the department store, Wolf stood casually on lookout as Snake jimmied the store's lock. As soon as they had the door open, the two slipped inside and began filling their bags with as many gifts as they possibly could.

Meanwhile, back at the radio station, DJ Trudy Tude droned into the microphone, "That was 'No No No Noel' by Death Anchor. *Bah humbug*, amirite?" She pressed a wah-wah button on her soundboard, just as Shark—who was dressed in the ultimate Scrooge costume—barged into the studio. Trudy Tude looked up in surprise. "Scrooge?"

She whispered. Then she shook her head and said, "Look, if you're here to teach me the meaning of Christmas, I'm not interested," she said, pressing her soundboard to make an old-time car horn sound blare out of the booth.

Shark blurted out in a weak British accent, "Don't you dare give the right dishonorable Ebenezer Scrooge the horn!" He waved his cane around in the air, trying to distract the bored DJ while also trying to push a specific button on her soundboard.

But Trudy Tude wasn't one to be easily fooled. "Buddy," she said, brushing his cane aside. "I don't work with side-kicks." She covered her mic, trying to keep Shark from getting a word in edgewise.

"I kick no one's sides," Shark said regally. "Unless it's that annoying brat Tiny Tim!" He jabbed his cane toward the board again, but just missed the button.

This piece of the plan was proving to be harder than Shark had expected . . .

CHAPTER EIGHT

Meanwhile, back across town, Wolf and Snake were ready to put the next part of their plan in action. They stood in front of a house, getaway car waiting patiently nearby, stuffed full of gifts they needed to distribute.

"This should be a breeze," Wolf said to Snake, as he gestured to the first house on their hit list. They were each holding a gift at the ready. "All you have to do is break into the house and leave a gift."

Snake hissed. He still did not like this piece of the plan. He was a *taker*, not a *giver*. But he'd do what he had to do to support their ultimate mission. "Fine. Let's get this over with."

Wolf watched as Snake slipped behind the house. Moments later, Snake was already back—without the gift in his hands. Snake muttered, "Welp, I definitely did it. We can go now."

Wolf eyed his buddy, who had a very boxlike lump stuffed into the center of his body.

"What?" Snake said, glaring back at him. "You never seen an ab before?"

"Cough it up," Wolf said, gesturing to the box hidden inside Snake's belly.

Snake grumbled as he hacked up the gift. And the vase he'd taken from the house while he was inside. Wolf shook his head. "Gimme a break," Snake muttered. "Giving, not taking, is unnatural."

With a sigh, Wolf said, "I'll do it. Watch and learn." He strolled confidently toward the house, returning mere moments later. "See?" he said, shrugging. "Piece of cake."

Snake nodded at something behind Wolf's back. "So, what's that, then?"

"What's what?" Wolf asked, in his most innocent-sounding voice.

Snake pointed to the present, which was hidden carefully behind Wolf's snazzy suitcoat. Wolf pulled the gift out from behind his back and looked at it, acting surprised that he hadn't actually completed his mission.

This fake-Santa business was a whole lot harder than it looked!

CHAPTER NINE

Back at the radio station, nothing was going according to plan, either. Though Shark had been certain his costume was spot-on, it didn't seem to be quite enough to distract Trudy so that Shark could execute his planned mission—to push that button. Trudy Tude chased Shark around the DJ booth as he tried and failed, again and again, to complete his part of the plan.

The DJ swung at him with a mic stand, but Shark was ready—he used his cane to swing back. Unfortunately, Trudy Tude's aim was so good that she managed to knock loose Shark's hat—ruining his disguise. Now he was just a shark with sideburns, swinging a cane.

With a gasp, Trudy Tude shouted, "Get ready to sign

off . . . 'cause I've been itchin' for a fight and you look a lot like that shark from the gang who took down Big Nick!"

Shark gestured to himself and said, "Me? No! I'm Scrooge. See? Muttonchops?"

Trudy Tude swung again, and this time her hit landed. She sent Shark rolling across the soundboard, and his big body pounded *all* the buttons as he rolled. Including a big, important-looking button with an antenna icon on it.

Up on the roof, Webs studied the computer she'd been working on to hack into the radio station. She frowned in confusion. "Shark," she said into her communication device. "Why did you cut the station's feed?"

"I didn't!" Shark wailed back into his communications unit. He dodged and weaved as Trudy came after him again and again. He was too big to hide, so he was stuck taking the full brunt of her attack. "Well, I *did*, but she made me!"

Webs launched into superfast hack mode, trying to

quickly figure out how to undo the damage Shark had done with the press of that antenna button. "The police channel is full of chatter about the station cutting out," Webs said hurriedly. "You've got to fill the dead air before they figure out what we're doing up here!"

Shark grinned and said, "Truly nothing I would love more, and I do have material prepared . . ." Then he ducked as Trudy Tude swung again. "But I kinda have my hands full here."

Piranha tapped Webs and said, "Patch me in, Webs."

Webs's eight legs kept *tap-tapping* even as she turned to look at her pal in confusion. "You? I mean—" She shook her head, entirely convinced this was not the right plan. "*You?*"

Piranha gritted his teeth. "Patch. Me. In." He shot her a steely nod, waiting for his cue.

With a shrug, Webs hacked quickly into the radio station's feed and nodded at Piranha.

On Webs's cue, Piranha broke into a spirited holiday song. He crooned and swayed, loving his moment in the spotlight.

Throughout the city, people quickly began to notice the jolly voice that was ringing out over the airwaves. The shaved-ice vendor stopped scooping for a moment and turned up his radio. People walking by slowed, then stopped, listening as Piranha's voice floated over the city.

Even Tiffany Fluffit, the chirpy but hardened news reporter, was wowed by Piranha's voice. From the site of the burnt-Santa-balloon building, Tiffany paused her reporting to listen in. Nearby, a tree full of holiday lights that had been off since the terrible balloon incident suddenly blared back on. The whole city instantly felt more festive than it had at any point since those peaceful moments before Santa went up in flames.

Piranha was really into his song now. And the emotion in his voice was obvious to everyone listening.

Piranha's Holiday Sing-along

Deck the city with balls of money
Fa la la la la la la la la!

'Tis the season to be heist-y
Fa la la la la la la la la!

Don we now our masks of bla-ack
Fa la la la la la la la la!

For all the loot goes in our sack
Fa la la la la la la la la!

Follow me in merry measure
Fa la la la la la la la la!

While I tell of yuletide treasure
Fa la la la la la la la la!

Deck the city with *BALLS OF MONEY!*
FA LA LA LA LA ... LA LA LA LA!

A shop owner stepped out of his front door to rehang a wreath he'd chucked into the trash that morning after the parade.

Inside the radio station, Shark and Trudy Tude had found their peace, too, and were now swaying together to the rhythm of Piranha's festive beat.

Thanks to Piranha's song, the spirit of Christmas was returning to the whole city.

Slowly but surely, this part of the plan was finally working!

CHAPTER TEN

Unfortunately, the other part of the Bad Guys' plan was still very much *not* working.

"Giving is hard!" Wolf grunted, trying and failing to drop the present he was holding. It was so hard to let go of it that Wolf wondered if it might be magnetically attached to his hand. As soon as he was able to pry one hand off the loot, his other hand reached out and grabbed it. "How does Santa do this?"

Snake sighed. "Yeah, it takes a real weirdo to let go of that much loot. C'mon, we'll do it together."

The two buddies headed back into the house, knowing they *had* to leave their gifts, or all the other parts of the new plan would have been for nothing.

Wolf and Snake slid into the house together.

Somehow, with a lot of pain and difficulty, they finally managed to drop the gifts and run. As soon as they were out, they fist-tail-bumped, then raced back to their gift-filled getaway car to grab more loot.

Baby steps.

It obviously wasn't going to get any easier to give rather than take, but this crew never gave up on a good plan. No matter how hard it was to get it done.

Meanwhile, back in the heart of the city, Piranha had started to run out of verses in his original Christmas tune. "*Doo wah doo*," he crooned.

At that moment, Webs hit the last keystroke on her computer and pressed play on her holiday playlist. The musical notes of favorite Christmas songs flowed out of speakers all over the city. Outside the building with the charred Santa face, even *Santa* suddenly looked a little jollier now that it sounded more like the holidays. As pedestrians wandered by, some folks paused to look up and wonder: *Is that burned-up Santa balloon* smiling?

"Is Christmas un-canceled?" Tiffany Fluffit barked into her microphone. "After the unexpected carols and some secret Santas leaving presents all through the city, holiday spirit is up. But is it enough to fill the Big Nick–sized hole in our hearts? Stay tuned to find out."

CHAPTER ELEVEN

The Bad Guys gathered on the roof of their secret lair later that night. "Nice going, Fin Bro!" Shark said, lifting Piranha into the air to celebrate.

But Wolf wasn't quite as ready to celebrate—yet. "What if it wasn't enough?" he said, unable to keep himself from worrying. "If folks don't stay home to celebrate tomorrow, we won't be able to clean the city out."

"Wolfie," Snake said soothingly. "It's late. We did the best we could. If not this year, there's always next."

But Wolf wasn't willing to give up. There was always more that could be done. "No," he said. "We—we just need something big to push holiday spirit in the city over the edge."

Shark smiled sweetly. "You can stop dropping hints now, Wolf," he said, nodding. "I'll do it. I'll perform my one-shark Christmas villains showcase. I don't know where I'm going to find twenty tons of fake snow on such short notice, but I'm a professional, so I'll find a way."

Wolf snapped his fingers. "Shark, that's it! If we made it snowy, the holiday spirit would be undeniable. There'd be no stopping us, then!"

"Finally," Webs whooped. She'd been waiting for someone to make this exact suggestion. It was her big moment. "A chance to hack the atmosphere! I actually have an app for that. We're good with a little collateral flooding, right?" She began to type away, preparing for the very hack job she'd been waiting to do.

"Or—" Wolf said, holding out a hand to stop Webs before she went too far with what was surely a disaster waiting to happen. "We just steal the snow machine at the ski resort."

The Bad Guys' Favorite Flavors of Holiday Shaved Ice

Shark: Blood Red Raspberry & Candy Cane Swirl

Snake: Guinea Pig Holiday Surprise Push Pop

Wolf: Jingle Bell Granny Grape

Webs: Ho-Ho-Holi-Fly

Piranha: Sea Salt Sugar Cookie

Piranha shook his head. "Even with your driving, we'll never get there and back in time."

Snake, who'd been gazing out over the holiday scene below, suddenly had a different idea. "What about that?" he said, nodding down at the shaved ice stand on the corner below.

Wolf grinned as he realized what his pal was suggesting. "We use the shaved ice machine to make snow!"

"Not *as* exciting as altering Earth's weather through atmospheric geoengineering," Webs said sadly. "But I think I could make it work."

CHAPTER TWELVE

It was, once again, Shark's time to shine. Dressed as a holiday shopper, bogged down with presents, he approached the shaved ice stand. Shark dumped a load of bags and packages onto the counter and the vendor held a few in his arms while Shark pretended to get organized.

"Thank you," Shark said gratefully. "I'm all turned around. First, Christmas is canceled. Now maybe it's back on? So, I'm rebuying everything."

"Uh, sure," the vendor said, struggling to keep Shark's packages from toppling. "What flavor can I get you?"

Shark made himself as big as possible and answered, "Please describe them to me in great detail while I interrupt with all sorts of unnecessary questions."

While Shark did everything in his power to keep the shaved-ice-stand vendor busy, Snake snuck around the back of the stand. He quickly picked the simple lock to open the stand's door, and then signaled to Wolf and Webs that the coast was clear.

The inside of the shaved ice stand was smaller than it looked from the outside. Wolf and Webs had to be extra careful as they tiptoed toward the ice machine. Though they moved as carefully as possible, Wolf accidentally brushed against a stack of paper cones, which tumbled messily all over the floor.

Just as the vendor began to turn to see what had caused the commotion, Shark blurted out, "Hmmm . . . does Mistletoe Mint taste more like *missiles* or *toes*?"

The vendor gave him a funny look. "Uh, it just tastes like mint."

The vendor began to spin around again, but that's

when Shark barked, "Please maintain eye contact with me at all times!" More gently, he added, "I require trust-worthiness from my frozen-delicacy suppliers."

As soon as she reached the shaved ice machine, Webs connected a technical device with a dial that spun from one to ten. She leaned toward Wolf and said, "When I give you the signal, turn the dial up. A five should do it."

Wolf nodded, watching as Webs climbed higher to finalize their setup on the roof of the shaved ice stand. She and Piranha quickly worked together to attach a flexible metal duct onto the roof of the stand, then pointed it toward the street. Webs nodded. "All set, Wolfie," she muttered into her communications unit. "Fire her up."

Doing as he'd been told, Wolf spun the dial to five . . . but then paused to consider if that was enough. If *five* was good enough, wouldn't *ten* be even better? "Nothing is going to get in the way of our Holiday Heist-tacular," he reasoned aloud. He spun the dial all the way up, and then quickly fled out the back door of the shaved ice stand.

CHAPTER THIRTEEN

Ice shavings immediately began to shoot out of the stand, blanketing everything nearby in a soft, fluffy, frozen white. People started to gather, curious about how this *snow* could possibly be falling in their usually hot city.

As more and more people crowded the area, Tiffany Fluffit raced toward the shaved ice stand, microphone at the ready. She grinned into the camera and said, "Tiffany Fluffit, reporting live from the scene of an unexpected winter wonderland. It may not be real, but what in this town *is*? In fact, it's never felt more like the holidays in the city. Christmas is officially back on!"

The camera panned over the crowd. Someone was making a snowball; others had their heads tipped to the sky to revel in the *wintry* weather and catch snowflakes on their tongues.

"We did it," Wolf mused, smiling as he took in the scene. "We really did it."

"It's beautiful," Piranha muttered.

Even Snake seemed impressed. "It makes me feel all warm inside. So merry and bright, like someone lit a candle in the cold cavern of my heart." He shook his head to clear away the annoyingly good mood. "I mean, if you like that sort of thing. Which I don't. I do not."

Suddenly, the vendor raced out of the shaved ice stand, screaming, "She's gonna blow!" A second later, the stand began to shake and shudder, and ice began to shoot out of the stand like missiles. The air grew colder, and Webs noticed that she could now see her breath forming a cloud around her. "That's not good," she mused.

"It's too cold!" Piranha wailed. All the nearby palm

trees had started to freeze solid, and one near the shaved ice stand suddenly shattered like glass.

It had gone from cozy winter wonderland to blizzard in less than a minute! "For a brief moment," Tiffany Fluffit said, her teeth chattering as she tried to report on the scene, "it looked like the holidays were back on. But that moment has passed. A frozen vortex is spinning out of control downtown. Will it suck in all surrounding life?"

The Bad Guys weren't sure what to do. Things had gotten totally out of control.

Had they really created a frozen vortex that could suck in all surrounding life? That was crazy talk. "That's not going to happen," Webs said confidently. "As long as you didn't turn the dial all the way up, Wolf."

Wolf looked left, then right, refusing to meet Webs's eyes. Finally, he shrugged and confessed, "I figured a ten would be twice the holiday spirit?"

"Come on!" Webs wailed.

Piranha wriggled as he said, "You're lucky my fins are frozen . . ."

"Why, I oughta—" Snake snarled.

"I'm too talented to die!" Shark sobbed, cutting Snake off.

"That vortex is about to suck in the whole city," Wolf told his pals. "We don't have time to be mad at me!"

"I'll *make* time," Snake said. "Everything was *fine*. But no, you had to go and push things too far! Like always!"

"I know! I'm sorry." Wolf's guilt ate at him as the ice and snow continued to swirl around them. "It's just . . . stealing with you all on Christmas morning is the highlight of my year. I—I got so wrapped up in making sure our Holiday Heist-tacular happened, that I put you all at risk. And that's the last thing I'd ever want to do."

The other Bad Guys wanted to hear him out, but it

was hard to hear much of *anything* over the sound of their own chattering teeth.

"Uh . . ." Webs said, a small, frozen tear forming. "That's gross."

"Get a life," Piranha muttered, trying to hide a smile.

"Those are theatrical tears," Shark said, trying to wave away Wolf's sweet words.

"Yeah, fine," Snake grumbled. "Whatever. But we better stop that machine, or it won't just be our Holiday Heist-tacular that's canceled. Webs, can't you, like, hack your device?"

Webs nodded slowly. "Oh, yeah, sure! Why didn't I think of that?" Then she narrowed her eyes and screamed, "Of course I can't hack it! You think I'd leave security loopholes in my own tech? The only way to stop it is to unplug it."

Wolf shrugged. "Then that's what we do."

All five of the Bad Guys tried to make their way toward the shaved ice stand to cut the power to Webs's machine. But the whipping winds sent them reeling backward instead of forward. Webs, Snake, and Piranha were all so light they were actually *thrown* through the air in the opposite direction. Even Wolf was no match for winds this strong and made no headway at all.

Shark was the only one of them who could stand up to the powerful winter wind. Fighting against the force of the icy vortex, Shark took one slow step after another toward the shaved ice stand. But then, just as soon as he got within fin's reach of the stand, he was sucked into the polar vortex and disappeared.

"Fin Bro!" Piranha yelped.

Seconds later, Shark was shot back out. Though he looked unhurt and he wasn't frozen solid, the icy wind *had* stolen his shirt.

Embarrassed, Shark screamed out, "Cover your eyes. Don't look at me!"

"If Shark's not strong enough to get there," Piranha said, eyes wide, "who is?!"

Webs grinned as she got a *very* good idea. "I know who."

CHAPTER FOURTEEN

"The situation has worsen—" Tiffany Fluffit said, her words cut off as her microphone got sucked into the polar vortex. She shivered, but gathered herself together to catch her cameraman's attention, when she noticed something huge lumbering toward them down the frozen street. "Are you seeing this?" she asked.

The camera zoomed in. It was Roboclaus! And settled in right behind the controls, in a seat where no one could see him operating the giant mechanical robot, was Wolf!

"No, not that way," Wolf yelped, desperately trying to get the hang of the controls as the mechanical Santa stepped from side to side, wobbling down the street. "How do I—?"

"You have to relax," Webs explained through her

communications unit. "The suit is intuitive. Don't force it. Just walk."

Was she saying that whatever *he* did, Roboclaus would do, too? It was starting to seem that way—because with each move Wolf made, Roboclaus followed suit.

"Folks," Tiffany Fluffit yelled into the camera. "We're witnessing some sort of Christmas miracle! A Santa *cyborg* appears to be attempting to save the city!"

Wolf began to relax, taking one step after another—until he'd almost reached the shaved ice stand! But as soon as he got almost close enough to touch it, the mechanical Santa's metal feet began to skid on the frozen ground. He hit the ground—hard. And then again—and again—and again. But Wolf wasn't about to give up. This was their only chance to make Christmas right again!

Suddenly, he looked down at the ground and noticed his friends were getting pulled closer and closer to the frozen vortex. They were gripping each other to keep any one of them from getting sucked in, but it was clear they wouldn't be able to keep safe for long. They needed Wolf! Now he was even *more* determined—his buddies were worth more than a million Holiday Heist-taculars! Wolf drew himself upright inside the giant mechanical suit and took another step forward.

Finally, he made it! He reached one long, metal arm forward—and grabbed Webs's tech device off the machine. The ice that had been whirling around them suddenly stopped, and the frigid vortex collapsed into nothingness.

The crowd around them roared with happiness. Everyone rushed toward Roboclaus and Wolf, who was still hidden high above their heads inside the control center of the huge mechanical Santa. Shark slipped on a quick disguise that made it look like he was Roboclaus's handler, and attempted to control the crowd. "One at a time, folks!" He cried out, trying to sound as in charge as possible. "Please form a line!"

While Shark distracted the crowd, the rest of the team worked quickly to get Wolf out of the suit before anyone figured out it was him who'd saved the day. They had a reputation as *Bad Guys* to uphold, after all . . .

From the scene of all the chaos and cheer, Tiffany Fluffit reported into the camera one last time, "Balloon Santa may have gone up in flames, but the city has a new Santa mascot: that's right, Roboclaus is a huge mechanical robot that *screams* family fun!"

As if on cue, Roboclaus shot flames out of his hand. The crowd screamed in terror—and then erupted in cheers. It really did scream fun!

CHAPTER FIFTEEN

Back at their getaway car, the Bad Guys watched as Tiffany and the crowds gathered around Roboclaus.

"I gotta hand it to you, Webs," Snake said, nodding his head. "They really love your Santa."

"Maybe too much," Piranha said, watching as people gave Roboclaus the same love and attention they'd earlier given to Big Nick, the giant Santa balloon. "These people gotta get home if we're gonna pull our Holiday Heist-tacular in the morning."

Webs pulled out her laptop and began to hack into the suit. She was able to operate Roboclaus like a giant puppet. She tried to make him wave to his fans, but again, fire briefly shot out of his hand instead. "Shark," Webs said, typing at her controls quickly. "I just patched your comms into the suit. He's no Scrooge, but think you can play Santa?"

Shark grinned and tested out his very best Santa voice. "Ho ho ho!" he boomed. "Happy holidays! Now it's late, so everyone go to bed. Because Santa commands that *everyone* celebrate tomorrow . . . in their homes and *not* at their security guard jobs!"

"I'll do it!" Gary the bank guard whooped. "I'll stay home for you, Roboclaus! Please be proud of me!" He tossed his security hat onto the ground and ran away from the bank as fast as he possibly could. Everyone else in the crowd also began to wander off, heading toward home to celebrate the holiday with their families.

"We did it!" Wolf said, shooting the Bad Guys a wolfish grin. "The Bad Guys saved Chrism—achoo!"

CHAPTER SIXTEEN

Sniffling, Wolf shuffled into the lair's living room the next morning. All his pals were slumped on the couches and chairs and floor, moaning and coughing and groaning. "I can't believe," Wolf said, stopping to sneeze again. "That after all that—*achoo*—we're too sick to pull off our Holiday Heist-tacular."

Snake whined, "How about a new tradition: No more traditions! Or holidays! *Bah humbug!*"

Shark squinted, looking suspiciously in the direction of the fireplace. "What. Is. That?" he muttered.

A pile of presents was gathered at the base of the chimney, wrapped in beautifully festive paper. "Oh no," Webs said, her eyes growing wide. "I think they're presents."

"Like, for us?!" Piranha yelped.

Horrified, Webs nodded. "We must have done so much good for the city, that we ended up on Santa's *Nice List*! I'm gonna be sick."

"The shame!" Shark wailed.

"Not only did that bearded freak have the gall to break into our lair, he goes and gives us *presents*, not *coal*?" Piranha cried. He leaned over to sniff a present, then perked up. "Wait—is that stinky cheese? How did he know?!"

Snake grumbled, "The Bad Guys will be the laughing-stock of the criminal community. I'll never be able to show my face again." He pulled down his ski mask to cover his face from the humiliation.

Wolf wiped his nose, then leapt toward the heist board. "This will not stand," he declared angrily. "We need to start planning *now*. Next year, we are going to heist the *North Pole* and show Santa that the Bad Guys *belong* on the Naughty List!"

Santa's Nice List

~~Wolf~~

~~Snake~~

~~Shark~~

~~Piranha~~

~~Tarantula (aka Webs)~~

And so, yeah.
The Bad Guys stole Christmas from ourselves, and
Santa deemed us good little elves.
Until next year, when we get all not nice . . .
Happy Heisting to all, and to all a good heist!

THE END

. . . or is it?

"Yo, Fin Bro," Piranha said through his communications unit. "You ready to roll?"

Shark adjusted his wig and tipped his top hat gently to one side. Then he tugged at the collar of the button-up silver shirt he'd stuffed himself into. "Ready and feeling *fine!*" he said. Wearing his disguise, Shark looked *just* like the famous musician—DJ Midnight—who had been hired to spin some tunes while the shimmery New Year's Eve ball dropped down from the ballroom's ceiling right at the stroke of midnight.

"New Year's Eve," Wolf snickered as he, Snake, and Piranha casually sauntered up the steps toward the famous New Year's Eve gala. "The night where we wrap up one year and start the next with some good old-fashioned heisting." It felt so good to be ending the year with one final heist—and this one was gonna be a *big* one. Their plan was to steal the diamond-studded New Year's Eve ball right out from everyone's noses during the big gala. "This ball is worth *millions*," Wolf said, grinning at Snake. "When we pull this heist off, we'll definitely be celebrities in the criminal world."

Snake slithered up the stairs, heading toward the giant front doors that opened up into the glitzy ball. "Let's do this," he said. "We get the goods and get out." There was no better party than a party that ended with a thrilling getaway chase.

Webs had already secured her position inside Shark's hat. She and her tech were ready to roll—all that was left was to get inside and get access to the main control panel backstage.

Wolf spun around just as a long, black limo rolled up to the curb. The door opened and out stepped Shark—looking and playing his part as DJ Midnight perfectly.

"Please!" Shark said, waving his fin at the crowd of

paparazzi who immediately swarmed around him. "Please, photos are fine—but no touching."

Shark spun and bowed and posed for a few glorious minutes, until Webs reminded him from inside the giant hat, "Uh . . . Shark? The point of your costume is to get us *in* to the party and get backstage. Not to stay out here and mug for the cameras all night."

Reluctantly, Shark waved to his adoring fans and continued his climb up the stairs. Once inside the party, he was immediately swept into the VIP lounge off the stage—which meant their plan was going exactly as they anticipated.

As soon as he and Webs were inside the glamorous suite, Shark barked out to the collection of waiters and less famous celebrities who were milling around the gently lit space, "I need total privacy before I perform! Everyone, leave this area at once, or I will not share the gift of my tunes with you tonight!"

Once they were alone in the suite, Shark popped off his hat and Webs jumped out. "Nice work. Now I'll head backstage and hack into the diamond ball's mechanical system while you keep up your performance back here."

Now that Shark's part of the plan was nearly complete, he was more than happy to take a few minutes to enjoy some of the tasty delicacies that had been laid out in the VIP suite. "Ooh! Caviar!" he said, scooping up a finful. Then he grabbed a plate of sushi and dumped that into his open mouth, too.

Meanwhile, Snake and Wolf slipped inside the party while Piranha—dressed in a dapper tuxedo and holding an important-looking clipboard—kept watch near the gala's front doors. The *real* DJ Midnight would be showing up sometime soon, and Piranha's job was to distract him and keep him from going inside. Snake and Wolf would be the lucky ones who got to actually nab the diamond ball.

Luckily, Piranha was the master of distraction. As soon as the DJ's limo rolled up to the curb, Piranha raced to open the door for DJ Midnight. But before Midnight could step out and make his way past the photographers and into the ball, Piranha hopped into the back of the car beside him. "Hey, hey!" he said to the startled DJ. "Name's Pir—Pirt. Yeah, Pirt. I've been tasked with the role of keeping you safe tonight. Unfortunately, we've gotten word that we need to take you in through a different entrance—around back. I assure you, this is only for your safety."

The DJ, who was wearing the very same silver shirt and top hat that Shark was sporting, nodded his head. "Yeah, yeah," DJ Midnight said, glancing down at his phone. "I expect total privacy before I perform, anyway. So that's cool with me." He nodded at Piranha and scowled. "*Total* privacy," he repeated.

"Gotcha." Piranha attempted to make himself as

small as possible, hiding behind a giant fur coat that was tucked into the limo's seat. "You won't even know I'm here. But my boss says I've gotta stay with you, by your side *all night*, to make sure we keep you safe."

"Fine, cool, whatever," DJ Midnight said with a sigh. "If you're gonna be looking at me all night anyway, can you at least help me warm up? Sing a few lines while I work out my beat?"

Piranha sprung out from under the coat and bounced joyfully on the seat. "It would be my absolute pleasure!"

With the *real* celebrity DJ taken care of, Snake and Wolf could move into their part of the plan. There were less than fifteen minutes until the stroke of midnight, and they had to act fast if they wanted to grab the ball and get out before everyone's attention was focused on it as they counted down to the New Year.

"Gentlemen," Webs said through her communications

unit a few minutes later. "Thanks to my superior tech work, the diamond ball will be unlocked from its platinum case and lowered a *liiiiittle* early this year—so as long as you're ready to go, you should be able to grab it before anyone even realizes it's within reach."

Just as Shark made his way onto the stage to pretend to set up for his set as DJ Midnight, the ball began its slow descent. From the dance floor, Wolf looked up and licked his lips while Snake grinned greedily beside him. They both folded into the fashionable crowd perfectly, with Wolf in his snazzy, shimmery green suit and Snake in a sharp tux with tails.

Everyone was so busy chatting and partying and gazing up at Shark onstage that they didn't even notice the dazzling diamond ball that was suddenly hovering in the air above their heads. Wolf knew this was his moment. He began to unleash a series of dance moves, urging everyone who was standing under the ball to clear the area—until he had a wide-open space in the center of the dance floor all to himself.

Wolf spun and wiggled his arms in the air, taking up as much space as possible. Just as the ball slipped even lower, so it was hovering right above his head, he hoisted Snake onto his shoulders and jumped.

Using Wolf's shoulders as a sort of springboard, Snake leapt onto the top of the ball and pulled out the tool he'd brought to cut the ball loose from its chain. He snipped, the ball dropped, and Wolf spun into position right below it so he could catch it and run.

What the Bad Guys *hadn't* bargained for, though, was how much several million dollars'-worth of diamonds *weighs*. So as soon as the ball dropped, Wolf was pinned down by hundreds of pounds of jewels—right in the center of the dance floor.

The crowd gasped and people began to point at Shark onstage and Wolf and Snake in the center of the dance floor. "Hey, it's the Bad Guys!" someone yelled.

Unfortunately, that's also when the *real* DJ Midnight finally realized he'd been tricked and came rushing onto the stage alongside Shark. He and Shark stared at each other for a second, before Shark tipped his hat at his twin and said, "Well, I'll leave you to it, then."

Just as the real DJ settled into his rightful place onstage, Shark leapt *off* the stage and shoved the diamond ball off his buddy. The ball rolled onto the hard dance floor . . . and that's when everyone heard something crackle. As that jeweled ball rolled lazily across the dance floor, diamonds plinked and snapped off and went skidding in every direction across the hardwood floor.

Shark offered Wolf a hand and pulled him up—but not before they each used their highly perfected pick-pocketing skills to scoop up a few shiny souvenirs from the dance floor along the way. It was time to get out of there. Their cover had been blown and even if they hadn't gotten the *whole* ball, they'd gotten some after-party goodies for the road . . .

While the clock struck midnight, Wolf, Shark, Snake, Piranha, and Webs ran from the gala and hopped into their getaway car—leaving the *formerly* diamond-crusted ball behind in the center of the party's crowd. What a shame that the ball was a whole lot less shimmery than it had been earlier in the night!

"Well," Wolf said as he steered through the city's streets under the shining streetlights. "Maybe it wasn't exactly a *perfectly* successful heist . . . but it *was* a fun way to end the year. And we're a little more sparkly than we were earlier tonight." He pulled a few of the diamonds out of his suitcoat pockets as police sirens sounded in the distance.

Even though they didn't have the diamond *ball* in the car with them, at least they had pockets full of loot—*and* they'd fulfilled Snake's wish to start the year with a good old-fashioned chase.

But even better than that was they had the rest of the year ahead of them, and they all knew there were lots more heists to be had. The Bad Guys were ready for the New Year!